"**Mr. Pendleton knew I like mysteries, right?**" Sarah-Jane said to Timothy and Titus. "So he gave me one. There's a secret message of some kind in this box. And it's not just for me. It's for you guys, too. That's why he put in the letters *T.C.D.C.*!"

Solve all the Beatitudes Mysteries along
with Sarah-Jane, Ti, and Tim:

# THE MYSTERY OF THE
# CANDY
# BOX

*Elspeth Campbell Murphy*
*Illustrated by Chris Wold Dyrud*

# Chariot Books™
David C. Cook Publishing Co.

A Wise Owl Book
Published by Chariot Books™,
an imprint of David C. Cook Publishing Co.
David C. Cook Publishing Co., Elgin, Illinois 60120
David C. Cook Publishing Co., Weston, Ontario

THE MYSTERY OF THE CANDY BOX
© 1989 by Elspeth Campbell Murphy for text and Chris Wold Dyrud
for illustrations.

Cover design by Steve Smith
First printing, 1989
Printed in the United States of America
94 93 92 91        5 4

**Library of Congress Cataloging-in-Publication Data**
Murphy, Elspeth Campbell.
   The mystery of the candy box / Elspeth Campbell Murphy;
illustrated by Chris Wold Dyrud.
        p.   cm.—(Beatitude mysteries)
   Summary: Sarah-Jane and her cousins investigate the mystery of a
box full of odd items, the legacy of an elderly man she befriended
before his recent death, and experience the meaning of the Beatitude,
"Blessed are the merciful, for they will be shown mercy."
   ISBN 1-55513-570-6
   [1. Cousins—Fiction. 2. Beatitudes—Fiction. 3. Mystery and
detective stories.] I. Dyrud, Chris Wold, ill. II. Title.
III. Series: Murphy, Elspeth Campbell. Beatitude mysteries.
PZ7.M95316Mw   1989
[Fic]—dc19                                      89-30009
                                                   CIP
                                                   AC

# CONTENTS

"Blessed are the merciful,
for they will be shown mercy."

*Matthew 5:7 (NIV)*

# 1
# LAST WILL AND TESTAMENT

A man dressed in a suit and carrying a briefcase got out of the car and came up the walk.

"Good morning," he said to the cousins, Timothy, Titus, and Sarah-Jane, who were raking leaves and jumping in the piles. "Is this the Cooper home?"

"Yes," said Sarah-Jane. "I'll get my dad."

"Well, actually," said the man, "I'm looking for a Miss Sarah-Jane Cooper. I'm an attorney, and I need to see her about a legal matter. Do you know where I might find her? Does she live here, too?"

Sarah-Jane stared at him. "I'm her."

At her side Timothy exclaimed, "A *lawyer*! Good grief, S-J! What did you *do*?"

The man laughed. "Oh, there's no problem, I

assure you. Though I must confess to being somewhat taken aback myself. I was expecting to meet an adult, that is to say, a grown-up. Miss Cooper—um, Sarah-Jane—has been named the sole beneficiary in a will. But because she is a minor, it seems I need to consult with Mr. and Mrs. Cooper after all. My name is Dan Taylor, by the way."

In the midst of all those words, Sarah-Jane picked up the idea that she had inherited something. That had never happened to her before in her whole life.

Titus asked the very thing they were all wondering about. "Does this mean Sarah-Jane is rich?"

"Um, no," said Mr. Taylor, looking uncomfortable. "No, I'm afraid not." Then he added, "I must say that this is the most unusual will I've ever handled. I'm afraid it will take a bit of explaining."

## 2
## FRIDAY'S CHILD

The cousins and Mr. Taylor and Sarah-Jane's parents all gathered in the living room.

"Now, then," began the lawyer. "No doubt you are all very curious as to who has remembered this little girl in his will."

"Yes," said Sarah-Jane thoughtfully. "I'm not really friends with any dead people. Except—"

But she couldn't go on, because Timothy and Titus had exploded into nervous giggles. "Not friends with any dead people!" they repeated, gasping because they were laughing so hard.

Sarah-Jane looked right at them, as serious and dignified as a teacher waiting for her class to come to order.

When Timothy and Titus had finally calmed

down, at least partway, she continued. "As I was going to say, except for old Mr. Pendleton, who was a very dear friend of mine."

She glanced at Mr. Taylor, who nodded to show that it was, indeed, Mr. Pendleton's will.

"I even went to his funeral and everything," Sarah-Jane added.

Mrs. Cooper put her arm around Sarah-Jane's shoulders. "Yes, it was your first funeral, Honey, and you handled it all very well. It was nice you wanted to go. Mr. Pendleton had no family and very few friends."

Something about the way Sarah-Jane looked or sounded got through to the boys, because they settled down almost all the way then. They looked at the carpet and muttered.

"Sorry, S-J."

"Yeah, sorry, S-J."

Then they moved so that they couldn't see each other and break up all over again.

Sarah-Jane appreciated that. She was surprised herself at how sad it made her feel just to hear Mr. Pendleton's name.

"So—who was he, anyway?" asked Titus nicely.

Sarah-Jane sat back, feeling a little better. "He was this old man who lived in a nursing home. And I used to go visit him on Friday afternoons. The deacons in our church asked if any Sunday school kids wanted to go visiting with them. I was one of the ones who signed up. At first it was kind of scary, because some of the people there are *so old*. But it's OK when you get used to it.

"Mr. Pendleton was my special favorite. And he called me his 'Friday's Child.' That's because

11

I came on Fridays and because of the rhyme that says, 'Friday's child is loving and giving.' It was nice of him to say that. But I didn't feel like I did all that much. I just talked to him. He liked to hear me talk. And he didn't call me a chatter-box—the way almost everybody else does.''

"So—what did you talk about?" asked Timothy, as nicely as Titus.

Sarah-Jane shrugged. "Stuff. You know, school stuff.

"And church stuff. Like, I told him about how we were trying to raise money for a children's mission hospital. And I showed him the thermometer chart I made. That's when you color it in red when you get some more money. We weren't anywhere near done. But I kept taking it to show him how far we were getting. And he would say, 'Have faith, Friday's Child. One day that thermometer will go right over the top.'

"And home stuff. Like, I told him about how I got to pick out material for my bedroom curtains at that new fabric store, Buttons 'n Bows.

"And I told him about you guys and our club and everything.''

12

"Oh, yeah?" asked Timothy. "What did he say?"

"He said, 'What's a teesy-deesy?' "

Timothy and Titus laughed again. But not wild giggles like before. It's just that everyone asked that same question.

"What *is* a 'teesy-deesy'?" asked Mr. Taylor.

"It's letters," explained Sarah-Jane.
"Capital T.
Capital C.
Capital D.
Capital C.
It stands for the Three Cousins Detective Club."

"Oh!" said Mr. Taylor as if he had suddenly figured out something puzzling. "Well, that might explain the Scrabble letters in the box. But it still doesn't explain the box."

And with that, Mr. Taylor opened his brief-case.

# 3

# THE MYSTERIOUS BOX

Sarah-Jane had been so involved in remembering Mr. Pendleton, that she had almost forgotten the will. But now she leaned forward, full of curiosity.

Mr. Taylor said to Sarah-Jane's parents, "As I've already explained to the children, this inheritance won't make your daughter rich. In fact, I'm afraid it doesn't amount to anything much at all. Just a box of keepsakes. Yet, Mr. Pendleton insisted that everything he owned should go to Sarah-Jane, because—and I quote—'She will know what I want her to do with it.' "

He turned to Sarah-Jane. "Does that message mean anything to you?"

Sarah-Jane shook her head.

"Ah, well," said Mr. Taylor. "I didn't think it would. I'm afraid Mr. Pendleton was rather eccentric."

"You mean crazy?" asked Titus.

"No, no," said Mr. Taylor. "Not crazy. Mr. Pendleton was certainly of sound mind. But he was—well, *unusual*; let's put it that way. He didn't do things the way everyone else does. For example—" Mr. Taylor paused and took a candy box from his briefcase. "*This* is Miss Cooper's inheritance."

Sarah-Jane recognized the box. It came from a wonderful new fudge store. The deacon and she had taken it to Mr. Pendleton. And Mr. Pendleton had been so nice about sharing. Suddenly her eyes filled up with tears.

Timothy and Titus jumped up to look over her shoulder as Sarah-Jane took the box from the lawyer. Taped to the top was a note in Mr. Pendleton's shaky handwriting. Titus read the note aloud. *"Blessed are the merciful, for they will be shown mercy."*

"That's one of the Beatitudes," said Timothy.

"But why did Mr. Pendleton tape it on my box?" asked Sarah-Jane.

Her father answered, "I think Mr. Pendleton put it there because that's how he felt about you, Sarah-Jane. To be *merciful* doesn't just mean to feel sorry for someone. It's more like you feel *with* him. It's like you get inside that person's mind and understand him from the inside out. When we understand people that well, we can be loving and giving and forgiving. And when we are understanding, people are more likely to be understanding right back. That's why the merciful are shown mercy.

"A lot of people just ignored Mr. Pendleton, because they thought he was a little odd. But you got to know him as a friend. And he got to know you. Now—aren't you going to open your box?"

Sarah-Jane grinned at her father and said, "Oh, well. If you insist."

Inside she found:

- a blue jay feather
- a little key
- two stones

- a bow tie
- a button
- a broken piece of a china elephant—just the trunk
- a thermometer
- a Santa's elf Christmas ornament
- the label from a honey jar with a big, red *2* printed in front of the picture of a bee
- four pieces from a Scrabble game—a *T*, a *D* and two *C*s

Mr. Taylor smiled gently at Sarah-Jane. "No doubt these items have a *special* meaning for you. Perhaps you would like to tell us why Mr. Pendleton left you these things?"

Everyone looked expectantly at Sarah-Jane.

But her voice was full of bewilderment when she said, "I don't have the slightest idea."

# 4
# A MESSAGE IN CODE

"Are you sure you don't know?" asked her father. "Could it have something to do with your *many* collections?"

"Yes," agreed her mother. "Didn't you often take your stuff to show Mr. Pendleton?"

Sarah-Jane nodded. "And no matter how much I took, he never called me a pack rat—like almost everybody else does. Except, he *did* say people shouldn't get too attached to *things*. 'Treasure in heaven, Sarah-Jane,' he used to say. 'That's the important thing. It's just as the Bible says. No point in storing up treasure on earth. No point at all. I did, and I'm sorry for all those wasted years.' "

"What treasure?" asked Timothy.

"Oh, I'm sure it was just a manner of speaking," said Mr. Taylor. "Mr. Pendleton lived in a tiny furnished apartment before he moved to the nursing home. What little money he had, went for his care. And he said that after he died his clothes should go to charity. All the rest is in that box. I'm sorry your inheritance doesn't amount to very much, Sarah-Jane. But at least you know he wanted to be remembered by his 'Friday's Child.' "

"I'll always remember him," Sarah-Jane said firmly. And it was as if she were making a promise to Mr. Pendleton himself.

Before Mr. Taylor left, he handed his business card to Sarah-Jane and said, "Call me if you have any questions."

Sarah-Jane put the card in the box.

After lunch, the cousins took the box into the family room and spread the contents out.

"You know what's strange about his collection?" Titus asked. Then he said, "It's not really a *collection* at all. A collection is a bunch of all the same kind of stuff. Like, I collect comic books. And Tim collects those metal buttons that he pins on his baseball cap."

"And I collect dolls," said Sarah-Jane.

"Among other things," said Timothy. He glanced around at Sarah-Jane's missionary postcards and souvenirs that had worked their way into the family room.

Titus said, "I suppose a person could collect different kinds of things that meant a lot to him. But what's so special about any of this stuff? I mean, these rocks aren't even pretty, so why would he keep them? And what's the point of having a key if it doesn't go to anything? Go figure."

"That's it!" exclaimed Sarah-Jane. She sat up, her eyes shining with excitement.

"*What's* it? What did I say?"

Sarah-Jane explained eagerly. "You said, 'Go figure.' That's what you do with something you don't understand. You figure it out. That's what you do with a puzzle or a code. You figure it out. Usually a code is written down. Only, *this* one is a code of *things*. Mr. Pendleton knew I like mysteries, right? So he gave me one. A secret message of some kind. And it's not just for me. It's for you guys, too. That's why he put in the letters *T.C.D.C.*!"

"Hey, yeah!" cried Timothy and Titus together. The box was even more interesting now that they knew it was meant for them, too.

The detective-cousins got right to work, trying to figure out the box of clues. They arranged the pieces every which way, putting them in different orders.

Nothing worked.

# 5

# QUAINT LITTLE SHOPS

Try as they might, the cousins couldn't make any sense out of a broken piece of a china elephant, a bow tie, two stones, a button, a thermometer, a feather, a key, a label from a honey jar, and a Christmas ornament.

They had started out eagerly, excitedly.

But they ended up cranky.

The boys were frustrated, but it was worse for Sarah-Jane. Timothy and Titus wanted to solve the puzzle. But Sarah-Jane wanted that even more than they did, because, to her, the puzzle was a message from a friend.

"Oh, I don't know," she muttered. "Maybe I was wrong about a secret message being in here. Or even if there is, who says I'll ever figure it out?"

Before the boys could answer, Sarah-Jane's mother appeared in the doorway. "Do you kids feel like getting out for a bit?"

"I guess so," said Sarah-Jane, still sounding pretty down. "Where are we going?"

"Well, I thought I'd go back to that new Buttons 'n Bows fabric shop," said her mother.

Instantly, Timothy fell on his knees and clasped his hands. "Oh, please, Aunt Sue! Not the fabric store! Pleeeeease! Anything but that!"

Titus joined in. "Yes, Aunt Sue! I can just see the headlines: *Nephews die of boredom*."

Sarah-Jane knew her cousins were trying to make her laugh. And it worked.

Mrs. Cooper laughed, too. "You clowns! It's not just a fabric store, is it, Sarah-Jane? There are all sorts of quaint little shops. Some Victorian houses along a little park were recently fixed up and turned into a kind of shopping center."

" 'Quaint little shops,' " repeated Titus wonderingly, as if he were a Martian, struggling to understand the ways of earthlings.

Timothy gulped as if he had just swallowed swamp water and said, "Sounds wonderful."

"Oh, come on, you guys," said Sarah-Jane. "You like fudge, don't you? There's a terrific fudge place. Roxie's Finest Fudge. They make it right there, and you can watch. So cool! Except you can't eat too much at one time, or you'll get sick."

"So what's their motto?" asked Titus. "*Eat Our Fudge and Get Sick Quick*?"

"Sounds wonderful," gulped Timothy.

Actually, the fudge was better than wonderful. Timothy and Titus were the first to admit that.

"Neat-O!" said Timothy.

"EXcellent!" said Titus.

But Aunt Sue made them stop before they were anywhere near sick.

The fabric store was in the same house as the fudge shop. It felt funny to be in a place that still looked like a house from the outside but that was all stores inside.

Upstairs there was a kind of crazy boutique filled with weird clothes. (At least Timothy and

Titus said they were weird. Sarah-Jane secretly thought all those feathers and sequins were very glamorous.)

There was also an all-year Christmas store. That looked interesting. But it was such a beautiful Indian summer day outside, the cousins didn't feel like Christmas yet.

So they wandered out to the little park and washed their sticky fingers in an old-time pump that really worked.

Then they went down the newly cobbled walkway and looked at the other houses that had been changed into stores. But they didn't need any stationery or needlepoint or fancy soap or candles or silk flowers. So they turned around and headed back.

"These houses are humongous," said Titus. "I guess people used to need lots of room for their big families and their servants."

"But these houses didn't stay just for one family," said Sarah-Jane. "They were divided up into little apartments, I think."

"Then what happened to the people who lived in the apartments?" asked Timothy.

"I don't know," said Sarah-Jane. "I guess
they all had to move someplace else."

The cousins walked back to the house where
the fabric store was and sat down on a little
wrought iron bench in the park. There was still
no sign of Sarah-Jane's mother, but that didn't
surprise them.

They sat back, admiring the sun on the col-
ored leaves and wondering what their chances
were of getting more fudge.

"Who dreams up the names for these
places?" said Titus, pretending to be disgusted.

(Actually, he liked making up names for things himself.) "I mean, just read the sign in front of the house. In this one place you have: a fabric store called *Buttons 'n Bows,* which makes sense, I guess. A fudge place called *Roxie's,* which makes sense, too, if that's the owner's name. And a Christmas store called *The Merry Elf.*"

"Which makes sense," chimed in Timothy and Sarah-Jane, laughing.

"And, to top it all off," said Titus, "A crazy boutique called *The Blue Feather*—"

He broke off and stared at Timothy and Sarah-Jane, who were staring back at him.

# 6

# CLUES, CLUES, CLUES

"A blue jay feather," said Sarah-Jane softly.

"Two rocks," said Timothy. "Not stones, rocks. *Roxie's.*"

"A button and a bow tie," said Titus. "*Buttons 'n Bows.*"

"And a Christmas ornament," said Sarah-Jane. "*The Merry Elf.* The things in my box are all the names of little stores!"

"But there were other things, too," said Titus. "What else was in the box?"

They closed their eyes tight, trying to remember.

It reminded Sarah-Jane of a game she had played at school parties. The teacher showed you a tray of objects. You were supposed to look long and hard and memorize them. Then the teacher hung a cloth in front of the tray and took away some of the things. When she showed you the tray again, you had to tell what was missing. It felt like that now. It was as if her friend Mr. Pendleton had given her a game to play. And somehow Sarah-Jane knew it was important to get it right.

"A thermometer!" she said. "I remember thinking that we already had our own thermometer, so we didn't need another one."

Timothy said, "You're right, S-J. I remember the thermometer, too. And a key. There was a key, remember? Ti said, 'What good is a key if it doesn't go to anything?' "

"That's right," agreed Titus. "I did say that. And I remember there was a broken elephant, too."

"*Part* of a broken elephant," corrected Sarah-Jane.

"*Part* of a broken elephant," repeated Titus. "That's right."

"Oh, and don't forget the honey jar label," said Timothy. (Timothy loved honey.) "There was something marked on it—a big figure *2*—in front of the picture of a bee."

Sarah-Jane thought for a moment. Then she said, "That doesn't sound right if you say it out loud. 'Two bee.' Shouldn't it say, 'Two bees'?"

Titus said, "How about, 'To be or not to be'?" But even he didn't think that made sense for the puzzle. "Oh, well," he added. "At least we remembered everything."

All three heaved a sigh of relief, sure that—yes—they had remembered everything that was in the box. But that comfortable feeling didn't last long when it dawned on them that they didn't know what to do next.

Then Sarah-Jane said they should check the other houses to see if there were any store names that had the words *key* or *elephant* or *thermometer* or *bee* in them.

There weren't.

Somehow the cousins hadn't thought there would be. But they checked anyway, because it felt like good detective work to do that.

"No, it's this house, all right," said Sarah-Jane when they came back. "This is where we're supposed to look."

"Look for what?" asked Timothy.

And for the second time that day, Sarah-Jane had to answer, "I don't have the slightest idea."

The cousins checked in at Buttons 'n Bows to see how Sarah-Jane's mother was getting along.

Mrs. Cooper was deep in conversation with a younger lady, who was asking her for sewing advice. Sarah-Jane heard the words "wedding" and "silk organza." She decided this was not the time to get her mother's attention and explain anything complicated—like about a box of clues having something to do with this house.

Mrs. Cooper smiled vaguely at the cousins and gave them more fudge money. (But not enough to make them sick.)

Timothy, Titus, and Sarah-Jane got their fudge. (Chocolate for Timothy, maple for Titus, and peanut butter for Sarah-Jane.) Then they sat down on the hallway stairs, nibbling their fudge to make it last longer, and tried to think.

They watched the mailman come in and begin filling the old-fashioned, fancy, brass mailboxes.

31

Just then a lady in a flowing skirt hurried downstairs. As she passed the cousins, she gathered up the folds of her skirt. "Horrors!" she said to no one in particular. "Children! With *fudge*!"

To the mailman she said, "I'm expecting some important mail. Do you have anything for The Blue Feather Boutique—2B?"

The mailman gave her a stack of letters, and she swept back upstairs.

But the cousins barely noticed her.

Another clue had just fallen into place.

They jumped up and ran out after the mailman.

# 7

# APARTMENT 2B

When they caught up with the mailman, the boys let Sarah-Jane do the talking, since the box of clues mostly belonged to her.

"Excuse me," she said, more breathless with excitement than running. "Have you been the mailman here for a long time?"

The mailman seemed surprised at her question. But he was nice.

"For quite a few years, I guess, why?"

"Well—because, before there were stores in this house, who used to live in apartment 2B?"

"Apartment 2B? Well, that would have been—Pendleton. Yes, Mr. Arthur Pendleton. Why? Do you know him?"

"He was a friend of mine," said Sarah-Jane. "But he died."

"Oh, I'm sorry to hear that," said the mailman. And the nice thing was—he really did sound sorry.

The cousins looked back toward the house and saw Sarah-Jane's mother coming down the front steps.

They rushed to meet her. This time the boys couldn't wait for Sarah-Jane to do the talking. All three started talking at once, explaining what they had figured out.

"Well, what do you know!" said Mrs. Cooper in amazement, when she finally understood what the kids were trying to tell her. "Mr. Pendleton used to have a little apartment in this house. I wonder how he knew you would figure that out?" She added with a smile, "Besides the fact that you're all incredibly smart, of course."

"He knew we came here," said Sarah-Jane. "Because—remember? I told him we came to the new fabric store, Buttons 'n Bows, to get material for my bedroom curtains. And the fudge I took him came from Roxie's. So he must have thought I would get it sooner or later."

34

"Well, you got it sooner," said her mother. "And I'm impressed."

That was nice to hear, of course. But Sarah-Jane still didn't feel satisfied.

Neither did her detective-cousins.

Titus said, "So—we know Mr. Pendleton wanted S-J to notice this house, where he used to live. What we don't know is—*why*?"

Timothy said, "And we still have three clues that we haven't used up yet."

As soon as the cousins got home, they made a beeline to the family room to look at those last three clues.

First they spread out all the clues they *had* used up:

A button and a bow tie for Buttons 'n Bows.

A couple of rocks for Roxie's Finest Fudge.

A Christmas ornament for The Merry Elf.

A blue jay feather for The Blue Feather.

Together those things stood for the house where Mr. Pendleton used to live before he went to the nursing home.

Then the cousins put the honey jar label next to the blue jay feather, because that stood for

apartment 2B. And 2B—where Mr. Pendleton used to live—was now The Blue Feather Boutique.

Sarah-Jane said, "I hope this doesn't mean we have to go back and talk to that lady. I don't think she likes kids."

"Horrors!" Timothy mimicked. "Children! With *fudge*!"

Titus grinned at him. Then he said seriously, "We might have to talk to her. But first we have to figure out what to ask her."

"Yes," said Sarah-Jane. "All we know is that

Mr. Pendleton used to live in the place where her store is now."

Titus said, "Do you suppose he put in the thermometer to show that he moved to the nursing home from there?"

Timothy and Sarah-Jane shrugged. It was possible.

Titus went on, trying to make other connections. "Thermometers make me think of hospitals or doctors' offices. Keys make me think of locked doors. Except this key looks too little for a door. Elephants make me think of a zoo or a circus."

Timothy added, "Or Africa. Or India. If we had the whole elephant, we could tell if it had big African ears or little Indian ears. It's too bad all we have is the trunk."

"A trunk," said Sarah-Jane softly. And something in her voice made the boys sit up and take notice. And they really took notice when she said, "Mr. Pendleton didn't mean *elephant*; he meant *trunk*. And it's a kind of joke, because he meant the *other* kind of trunk. *The kind you open with a key!*"

The cousins rushed to tell Sarah-Jane's parents about their new discovery. Mr. Cooper said, "Let me get this straight. You think Mr. Pendleton left you a message in code that says there's a trunk in the house where he used to live—and that you have the key to the trunk?"

Sarah-Jane nodded, hardly daring to breathe.

Mr. Cooper turned to his wife. "What do you think?"

"Well," said Mrs. Cooper. "Knowing Mr. Pendleton, anything's possible. I think leaving Sarah-Jane a box of clues is just the kind of thing he would do. And I think the T.C.D.C. might well be onto something."

"It's worth looking into," Mr. Cooper agreed.

He turned back to Sarah-Jane. "Here's what we'll do. You call Mr. Taylor, the lawyer. Tell him everything you told us. Ask him to meet us at The Blue Feather Boutique. We'll see if we can find this trunk."

Sarah-Jane had never called a lawyer before. Titus held the box of clues nearby in case she had to remember anything. And Timothy read the phone number from the business card.

Mr. Taylor wasn't at the office, so Sarah-Jane tried him at home. This time Timothy held the box, and Titus read the number.

Mr. Taylor seemed a little surprised to hear from her. Sarah-Jane thought that probably when he had told her to call if she had any questions, he didn't really think there would be any. But he was very nice. And he listened carefully.

He said the same thing as Sarah-Jane's father. "Well, it's definitely worth checking into. I'd be glad to meet you at The Blue Feather." Then he added, "Sounds like fun!"

As she hung up, Sarah-Jane suddenly realized she had already been having fun. Sure, the puzzle was hard. And sure, it had been frustrating.

But most of all, it was fun.

And then Sarah-Jane realized something else. Mr. Pendleton had had fun putting the whole thing together for her. She was sure of that.

To her cousins' surprise (and her own surprise) Sarah-Jane started laughing and crying all at the same time, as she packed up the box to take with her. Her funny, dear old friend had left her what she loved best—a mystery to solve. And she almost had it. Almost.

# 9

# AT THE BLUE FEATHER

The lady from The Blue Feather Boutique looked up in amazement as the three adults and three kids crowded into her little store.

She peered at the cousins and said, "Oh, dear. It's the fudge children."

"Yes," said Sarah-Jane. (Everyone had already decided that since it was Sarah-Jane's trunk—if there really was a trunk—she should do the talking.) "I'm Sarah-Jane Cooper. And these are my cousins—Timothy Dawson and Titus McKay. And these are my parents. And this is Mr. Taylor. He's a lawyer."

The lady clasped her hand over her heart and exclaimed, "My dear child! It's true I don't exactly welcome children into my boutique. But you didn't have to bring your attorney!"

Timothy and Titus looked at each other and rolled their eyes. Sarah-Jane knew what they were thinking, and she agreed with them. This lady certainly had a wacky sense of humor.

But Sarah-Jane had serious business. She said politely, "I came to get something. It belonged to a man who used to live here. But now it belongs to me."

"Well, I can't imagine what that would be. . . ." The lady thought for a moment. "Oh! Unless you mean that shabby old trunk?"

"YES!" cried the cousins together.

The lady looked startled. "Oh! Well, then. Let's see. As I understand it, the old man asked his landlady to put it in storage for him. And she asked me. But honestly, darlings! Do you see any storage place around here?" She waved her hand airily at the crowded racks and shelves.

Sarah-Jane could hardly get the words out. "So—so does this mean you don't have it anymore?"

"Oh, not to worry, my angel! I simply meant that I don't have it *here*. No, I tucked it away in that ghastly attic. Just go along the back cor-

ridor, through the little door, and up those dreadful stairs.''

From that description, Sarah-Jane was glad she didn't have to go alone. But with her two cousins and three grown-ups, she had all the excitement and none of the scariness. She even felt sure enough of herself to lead the way.

The stairs were creaky, and the attic was dusty, but it wasn't *that* bad. Sarah-Jane decided that anyone who sold feathers and sequins probably liked to exaggerate.

They found the trunk over against the wall by

the window. There was enough light to see a nameplate on it. Timothy and Titus wiped the dust away. It said: *Property of Arthur Pendleton.*

Mr. Cooper said in an overly serious voice, "What do you want to do, Sarah-Jane? Take it home first? Or open it now?"

Sarah-Jane knew her father was really kidding, because how in the world could she wait? Obviously her cousins felt the same way. She heard them mutter, "Come on, S-J! Come on, come on, come on! What are you waiting for?"

Sarah-Jane's hands were shaking as she tried the key in the lock.

It fitted perfectly.

# 10
# THE FINAL CLUE

As Sarah-Jane swung back the creaky lid, everyone crowded around to look into the trunk.

For a moment, no one said a word. They just stared in disbelief. They had never seen so much money in one place before.

"You hear about this happening," said Mrs. Cooper wonderingly. "Someone you never thought had money turns out to have stacks of it."

"But why is it here?" asked Titus. "Why did he put it in a trunk instead of a bank? Or why didn't he buy stuff with it?"

Mr. Cooper said, "Maybe he liked *having* money more than *spending* it. Maybe he liked having it near him. Then one day he realized

that it didn't matter to him anymore—and he didn't know what to do with it."

Mr. Taylor said, "I see I was wrong when I said Mr. Pendleton just used 'treasure' as a figure of speech. When he told Sarah-Jane about the *treasure* he had stored up, he meant real treasure."

"Yeah," said Timothy. "And the box of clues was like a treasure map. We were on a treasure hunt this whole time."

Titus asked, "Does this mean Sarah-Jane is rich?"

46

Mr. Taylor answered, "We'll have to count the money, of course. Most of it seems to be in small bills. But two things we know for sure: There's a lot. And it all belongs to Miss Cooper."

"No, it doesn't," said Sarah-Jane. She had been quiet all this time, thinking hard.

They all turned to stare at her.

She explained, "I know the money is not for me, because there's one more clue, remember?"

She reached in the box and pulled it out.

"The thermometer!" said Timothy and Titus together.

Sarah-Jane said, "Mr. Pendleton said in his will that I would know what he wanted me to do with—with whatever there was. And I do. Because—remember? Every Friday I used to take my missionary fund thermometer to show him how we were doing. And we'd talk about how much money we still needed to collect for the children's hospital. And he would say, 'Have faith, Friday's Child. One day that thermometer will go right over the top.' So that's why I'm positive Mr. Pendleton meant for me to put this money in the mission fund. Right?"

Sarah-Jane's parents put their arms around her.

Her mother said, "Yes, Sweetheart. We think you're exactly right. You understood Mr. Pendleton, and he understood you."

Her father said, "You showed mercy to each other. And together you'll be showing mercy to mission children."

Sarah-Jane carefully put the thermometer back in the box. The last clue had been figured out. The mystery was solved. And people could call her a pack rat all they liked, but she knew she would keep Mr. Pendleton's box of clues forever.

"Well," said Mr. Taylor briskly. "This calls for a celebration."

But Timothy and Titus were way ahead of him. They charged down the attic stairs, calling, "Fudge for everybody!"

**The End**